Other Schiffer Books By The Author:

The Sweet Rot, 978-0-7643-3406-1, $16.99

The Sweet Rot, Book 2: Raiders of the Lost Art, 978-0-7643-3828-1, $19.99

Library of Congress Control Number: 2011942118

Type set in Eraser

ISBN: 978-0-7643-3977-6
Printed in China

Schiffer Books are available at special discounts for bulk purchases for sales promotions or premiums. Special editions, including personalized covers, corporate imprints, and excerpts can be created in large quantities for special needs. For more information contact the publisher:

Published by Schiffer Publishing Ltd.
4880 Lower Valley Road
Atglen, PA 19310
Phone: (610) 593-1777; Fax: (610) 593-2002
E-mail: Info@schifferbooks.com

For the largest selection of fine reference books on this and related subjects, please visit our website at **www.schifferbooks.com**
We are always looking for people to write books on new and related subjects. If you have an idea for a book, please contact us at proposals@schifferbooks.com

This book may be purchased from the publisher.
Include $5.00 for shipping.
Please try your bookstore first.
You may write for a free catalog.

In Europe, Schiffer books are distributed by
Bushwood Books
6 Marksbury Ave.
Kew Gardens
Surrey TW9 4JF England
Phone: 44 (0) 20 8392 8585; Fax: 44 (0) 20 8392 9876
E-mail: info@bushwoodbooks.co.uk
Website: www.bushwoodbooks.co.uk

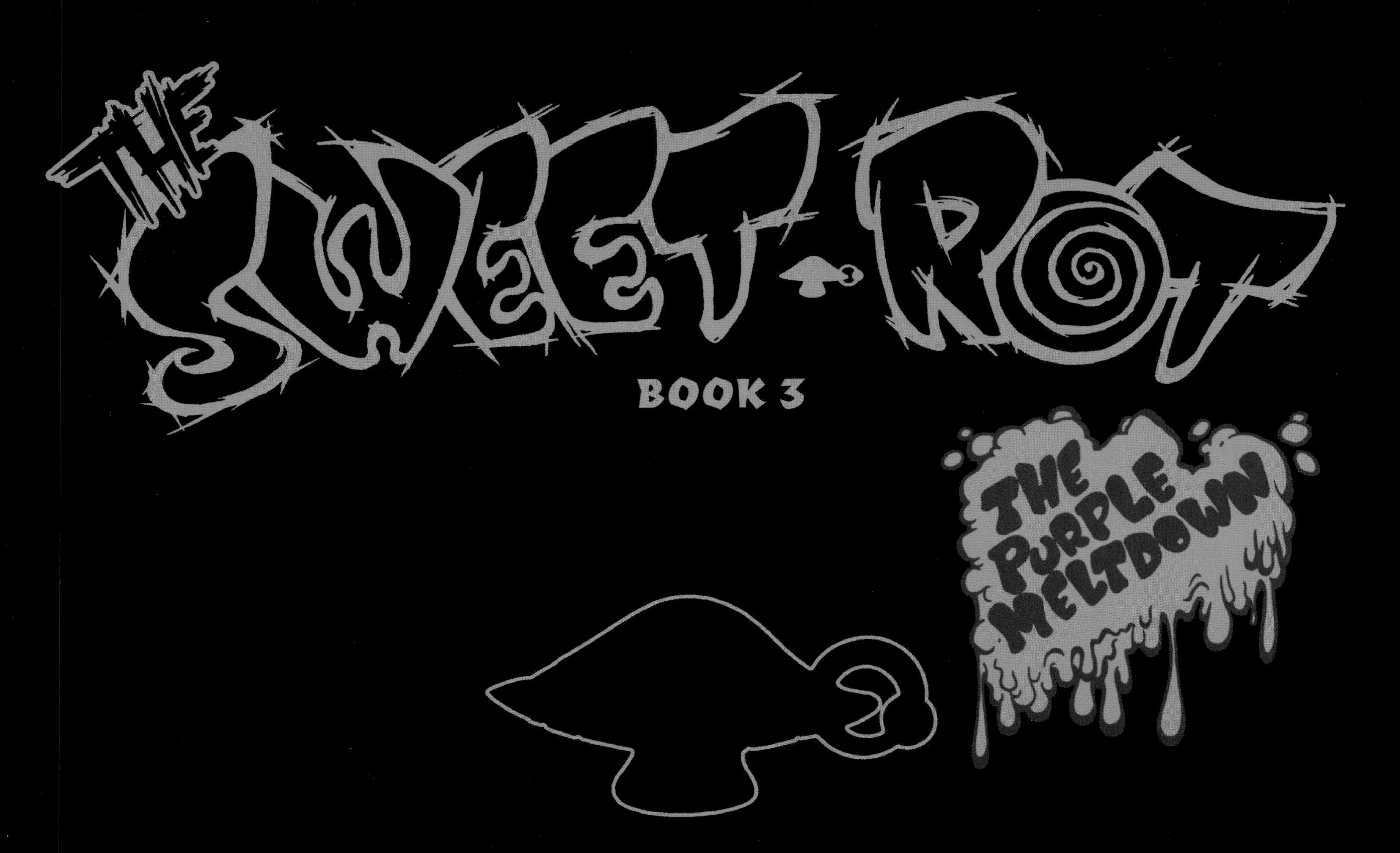

WRITTEN AND ILLUSTRATED BY JOE SIMKO

POLLILOP DROP HOLDS A CREW FOR THE NEW,
A TOWN ABOUT AROUND
A FEW HUNDRED ROTTERS OR TWO.
ONE SUCH MELLER-DWELLER, LITTLE ROTTER, POLLI-DROPPER
SPENDS HOURS CRAFTING POWERS AND SELLS SPELLS
WITH HER BLACK STUFFED KITTY NAMED "ROWRERS."

The BRAIN DRAIN
ART GALLERY
PUNK PIZZA
THE STITCH MIX

MYSTIC MIZ IS HER NAME,
A TAROT CARD EXPERT IN THE ASTROLOGICAL GAME.
FITCHEDY WITCH GIRL, BUT NOT A WITCH GIRL LIKE THE SAME.
THIS SPELL POPPER IS A DEATH STOPPER.
MYSTIC MIZ'S MAGICK ENDS TRAGIC
FOR OTHER ROTTERS IN PAIN.

STAR CHARTS

SO UPSET, FOR YOU SEE, WHEN ONE DAY SHE BELIEVED,
THROUGH HER CLASSIC GLASSIC ORBAGE A FORESIGHT WAS TEE-TEASED.
A TOWERING TOXIC PURPLE WAVE GRAVE
GAVE NO SPARE LIFE TO THOSE IT ENCAVED.
SPLISH TO THE SPLASH, OCEATIC AFTERMATH,
LILAC-ATTACK WITH NO WAY TO BE SAVED.

POLLILOP
DROP

THIS VIOLET VIOLENT VISION WAS LITTLE MYSTIC MIZ'S MISSION
TO WARN ALL THE ROTTERS THAT A PLUM-DRUM DOOM WAS NIGH.
CRASH SHE DID DASH OUT HER FRONT DOOR AND INTO TOWN SHE DID FLY.
NEARBY, PUKEBOY SHROOM SAT,
ROCKING KNOTTED NOTES FOR HIS ROTTED BLOKES,
JUST AS MYSTIC MIZ RACED FEVEROUSLY BY.

"WHAT'S THE HURRY, MYSTIC MIZ?"
PUKEBOY SANG IN A WAY THAT WAS HIS.
MIZ QUICKLY EXPLAINED, "WE'RE ALL DOOMED FROM A VISION GLOOM
I FORESAW IN MY CRYSTAL BALL!
WE MUST FIND A WAY TO STOP A PURPLE MASSIVE MELTDOWN TODAY!
WHAT COULD IT BE? MY FOREVISION CAN NO LONGER SEE!"

"HMMMMM..." MAUTRUSE THOUGHT.
"PERHAPS MY SCIENCE LAB IS CAUSE OF THIS DISASTER.
MY TEST TUBES, MIXING RED AND BLUES, WILL SURELY ERUPT A PURPLEY HAZARD.
I MUST GO BACK TO CHECK THAT MY CHEMICALS ARE PROPERLY SET,
AND POLLILOP DOES NOT POP AN ATOM BOMB RAPTURE."

MAUTRUSE
LABORATORY
EXPLOSION PROOF

GERF GULPED THE LAST DROP OF HIS LICKWATOX SHOT
AND SUGGESTED INSTEAD THAT THE PURPLE MELTDOWN AHEAD
MIGHT COME FROM A VIDEO ARCADE CABINET TOP.
"IT COULD BE A NEW VIDEO GAME CALLED 'THE PURPLE MELTDOWN.'
WHEN YOU LOSE, A GOO OOZE WILL POUR DOWN ALL AROUND,
BURNING YOUR HEAD, DISSOLVING YOUR ORGANS, AND CAKING YOU DEAD!"

THE PURPLE MELTDOWN
THE PURPLE MELTDOWN
THE PURPLE

"PSSSH-NAH!" SHOT SLUNKER WITH A ZJIP TO THE ZJOP.
HE SUGGESTED A DIFFERENT TAKE THAT WAS SURELY FULL OF FLOP.
"MAYBE SPACE CREATURES WITH DRIPPING FEATURES
WILL INVADE OUR POLLILOP DROP TOWN,
BLASTING SHIP-SHAPED SHOTS OF GRIP-GRAPED DROPS,
MELTING US LITTLE ROTTERS, ONE AND ALL TO THE GROUND!"

"SURELY THAT CAN'T BE IT," CLAIMED CANDY MAKER-BAKER RIZZLE BLITZ.
"PERHAPS MY CANDY FRUCTOSE FACTORY PIPES
WILL SPEW COLORED FUMES FROM MY NEW GUMMIE GOONS,
FORCING CUMULUS CLOUDS WITH SUGARED STOMACH PAIN.
A BURNING ACIDIC DRAIN WILL LEAVE POLLILOP DROP
WITH NO PRINCE TO SAVE US FROM THIS POLLUTED PURPLE RAIN."

"FORGET THESE MAYBES WHAT-IFS," FLOPPED PROPHET O' DOOM ROTTER RAGABOOM.
"THIS DISASTROUS PURPLE GOOP-DROOP
IS PROBABLY ALREADY INSIDE US, FULL OF VORACIOUS GUST!
AORTIC ARTERY AGONY AND PAINED VEINS FULL OF PURPLEACIOUS RUST!
BOILING IN OUR INNARDS, BUBBLING TO 'SPLODE,
SOON WILL BE SLUSH GUSHING OUT OUR EYES, OUR EARS, AND OUR NOSE!"

"We must stay collected and cooled," calmed Pukeboy to the kids.
"Building up fear is not a way to help get it rids.
A worry thought will only taunt, for I know what it did.
My own fear of playing guitar here bred it's strife.
We must not let this rot-threat kill our hot-breath of good life."

THE

STILL WORRIED OF WORLD ENDING, MYSTIC MIZ WANTED TO FIX.
PUKEBOY TO PACIFY, TOOK MIZ TO CHILL NERVES AT THE PUB CLUB STITCH MIX.
AS THEY THOUGHT OF THE MELTDOWN'S MEANING AND IT'S PURPLELYPTIC PURPOSE,
RIBBY RUB THE BARTRESS POURED LICKWATOX SHOTS AT THE BAR,
AND LITTLE BLOOP-A-TOOP PLAYED WITH HIS TOY FIGURES AND TOTALED TOY CAR.

FIREBLEED
LICKWATOX
SHROOM JUICE
SCREAMSICLE DRINK
THE STICKY MIX
SAVAGE COMICS

JUST THEN, GLITTER-SPITTER MIXEL MAZE DANCED BY IN A SWITCHED TWITCH OFF THE CLUB DANCE FLOOR AND TOWARD THE BAR OF STITCH MIX. AN ACCIDENTAL TRANCED-DANCE AND BONK-ZONK DID MIXEL MAZE BIDDY BAM, KNOCKING MIZ'S DRINK RIGHT OUT OF HER HAND.

"AHH," SMILED PUKEBOY. "YOUR MELTING MAUVE MASSACRE VISION, MASSIVE AND GRAND,
IS SIMPLY GROSS GRAPE LICKWATOX DRINK DROWNING BLOOP-A-TOOP'S TOY LAND."
MYSTIC MIZ WITH RELIEF, BREATHED WITH BELIEF.
THAT ANY TALL WORRIES SHOULD BE TAKEN AS SMALL FLURRIES,
THIS WAS AGREED AS BLOOP PLAYED IN THE NEWLY FORMED BLOBBED BARRIER REEF.

POLLPLOP DROP

THE END